2

D1337022

My First...
Baby Brother

First published in the UK in 2009 by
QED Publishing
A Quarto Group Company
226 City Road
London EC1V 2TT
www.qed-publishing.co.uk

A catalogue record for this book is available
from the British Library.

ISBN 978 1 84835 163 9

Author Eve Marleau
Illustrator Michael Garton
Consultants Shirley Bickler and Tracey Dils
Designer Elaine Wilkinson

Publisher Steve Evans
Creative Director Zeta Davies
Managing Editor Amanda Askew

Printed and bound in China

The words in **bold** are
explained in the glossary
on page 24.

My First...

Baby Brother

Eve Marleau and Michael Garton

QED Publishing

Every morning, Lizzie eats her breakfast with Mum, Dad and Max the dog.

4

"Mum, how long have you been **pregnant**?"

"Nearly nine months, Lizzie. The baby will be born any day now."

"I should make some room at the table!" says Lizzie.

Lizzie helps Mum to wash up after breakfast.

"Where will the baby sleep, Mum?"

6

"The baby will sleep in a **cot** in my room, just like your dolly's cot. When the baby is older, he will sleep in a bed, just like you."

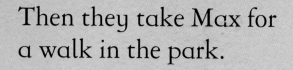

Then they take Max for a walk in the park.

"Will the baby want to play fetch with Max and me?"

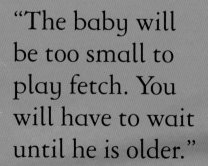

"The baby will be too small to play fetch. You will have to wait until he is older."

"Until then, you can spend time together in other ways. You can sing to him and tell him all about your day."

"Babies love their BIG sisters and brothers ever so much."

9

One day, Gran comes to
pick Lizzie up from school.

"Mum and Dad have gone to the **hospital**. It won't be long now until your baby brother arrives!"

11

Lizzie is outside in the garden with Grandad when Dad arrives.

"Dad! Dad!"

"Is my new brother here?
Where's Mum?"

"Yes, they are both at the hospital. Would you
like to come with me to meet your new brother?"

13

They go to the hospital to see Mum.
There is a tiny baby in
the cot next to her.

14

"Hi Lizzie. This is your brother, Charlie.
Would you like to say hello?" asks Mum.

Lizzie looks into the cot.
"I'm your BIG sister!"
she tells Charlie.

The next day, Mum
and Charlie come
home from the hospital.

16

"Can I do anything to help, Mum?" asks Lizzie.

"Yes, it's time for Charlie's bath."

Mum shows Lizzie how to make sure the bath water is just the right **temperature** for Charlie.

Then Gran and Mum put Charlie
down for a sleep in his cot.

18

Lizzie put a
blue bunny
in next to him.

"This is a present
from me, Charlie!"
whispers Lizzie.

Later, Lizzie hears Charlie crying. She goes into the bedroom.

"Why is he crying, Mum?" she asks.

20

"Charlie is very hungry after his sleep."

"What does Charlie like to eat?" asks Lizzie.

"He only drinks special milk for the first few months.
The milk has everything Charlie needs to grow."

21

Every morning, Lizzie likes to help Mum.

She helps to change Charlie's nappy.

She dresses him.

She plays with him.

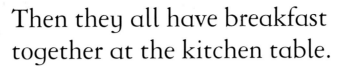

Then they all have breakfast
together at the kitchen table.

23

Glossary

Cot A baby's bed.

Hospital A building where people see doctors for medical treatment.

Nappy A piece of material that is wrapped around a baby's bottom to absorb and hold waste.

Pregnant When a woman or a female animal has a baby growing inside her.

Temperature How hot or cold something is.